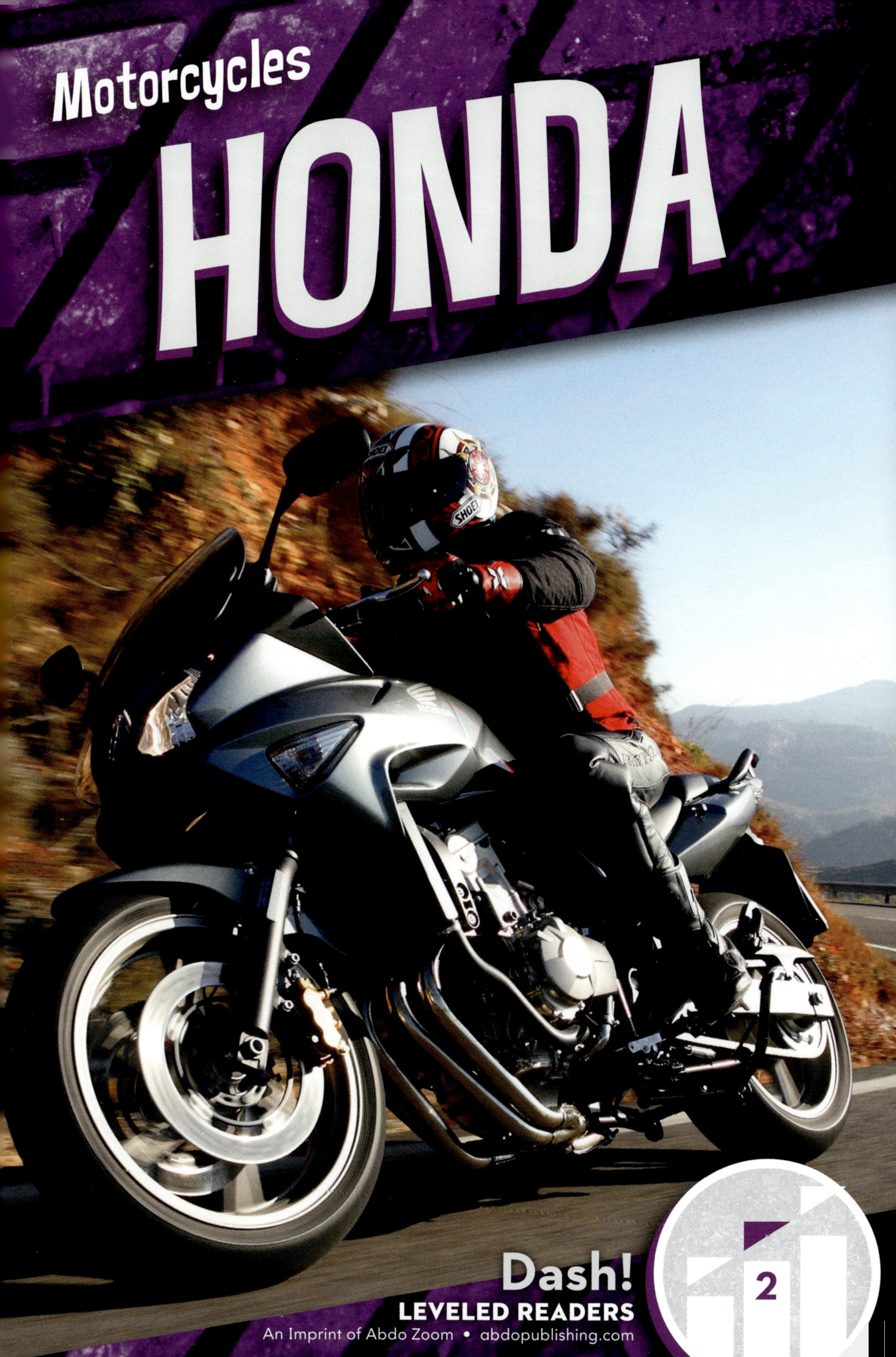

Motorcycles
HONDA
Dash!
LEVELED READERS
2
An Imprint of Abdo Zoom • abdopublishing.com

Level 1 – Beginning
Short and simple sentences with familiar words or patterns for children who are beginning to understand how letters and sounds go together.

Level 2 – Emerging
Longer words and sentences with more complex language patterns for readers who are practicing common words and letter sounds.

Level 3 – Transitional
More developed language and vocabulary for readers who are becoming more independent.

abdopublishing.com

Published by Abdo Zoom, a division of ABDO, PO Box 398166, Minneapolis, Minnesota 55439.
Copyright © 2019 by Abdo Consulting Group, Inc. International copyrights reserved in all countries.
No part of this book may be reproduced in any form without written permission from the publisher.
Dash!™ is a trademark and logo of Abdo Zoom.

Printed in the United States of America, North Mankato, Minnesota.
052018
092018

Photo Credits: Alamy, Getty Images, Glow Images, iStock, Shutterstock, ©Rikita p.6/CC BY-SA 3.0,
    ©Dennis Bratland p.12/CC BY-SA 4.0
Production Contributors: Kenny Abdo, Jennie Forsberg, Grace Hansen, John Hansen
Design Contributors: Dorothy Toth, Neil Klinepier

Library of Congress Control Number: 2017917514

Publisher's Cataloging in Publication Data

Names: Murray, Julie, author.
Title: Honda / by Julie Murray.
Description: Minneapolis, Minnesota : Abdo Zoom, 2019. | Series: Motorcycles |
    Includes online resources and index.
Identifiers: ISBN 9781532123047 (lib.bdg.) | ISBN 9781532124020 (ebook) |
    ISBN 9781532124518 (Read-to-me ebook)
Subjects: LCSH: Honda motorcycle--Juvenile literature. | Motorcycles--Juvenile literature. |
    Bikes--Juvenile literature. | Honda Motor Company--Juvenile literature.
Classification: DDC 629.22750--dc23

Table of Contents

Honda
HONDA

Honda is a Japanese motor company. It was started by a man named Soichiro Honda.

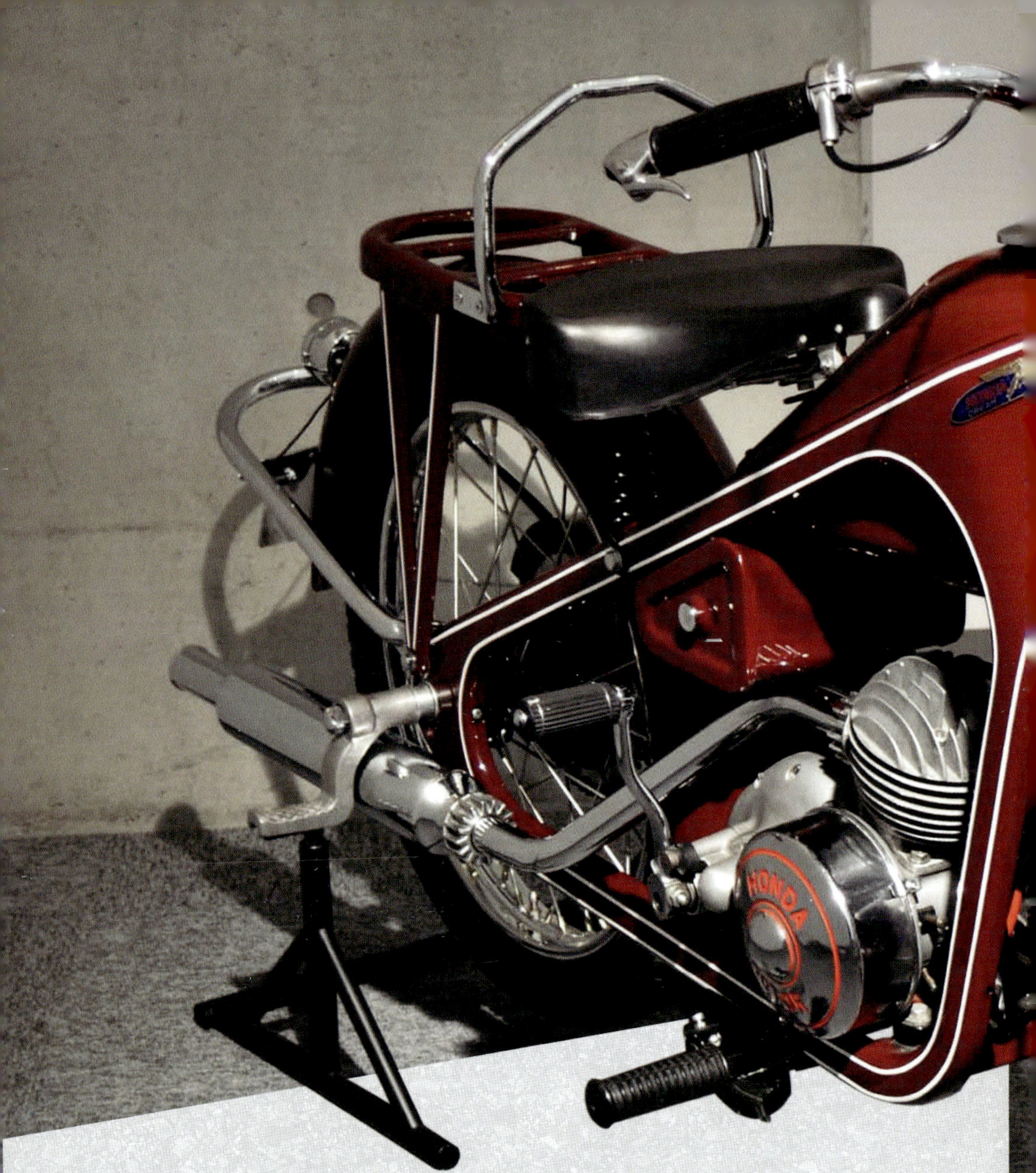

The first Honda motorcycle came out in 1949. It was called the D-Type. The D stood for Dream.

In 1958, Honda came to the United States. The C100 Super Cub was the first motorcycle sold. It was the best-selling motorcycle of all time.

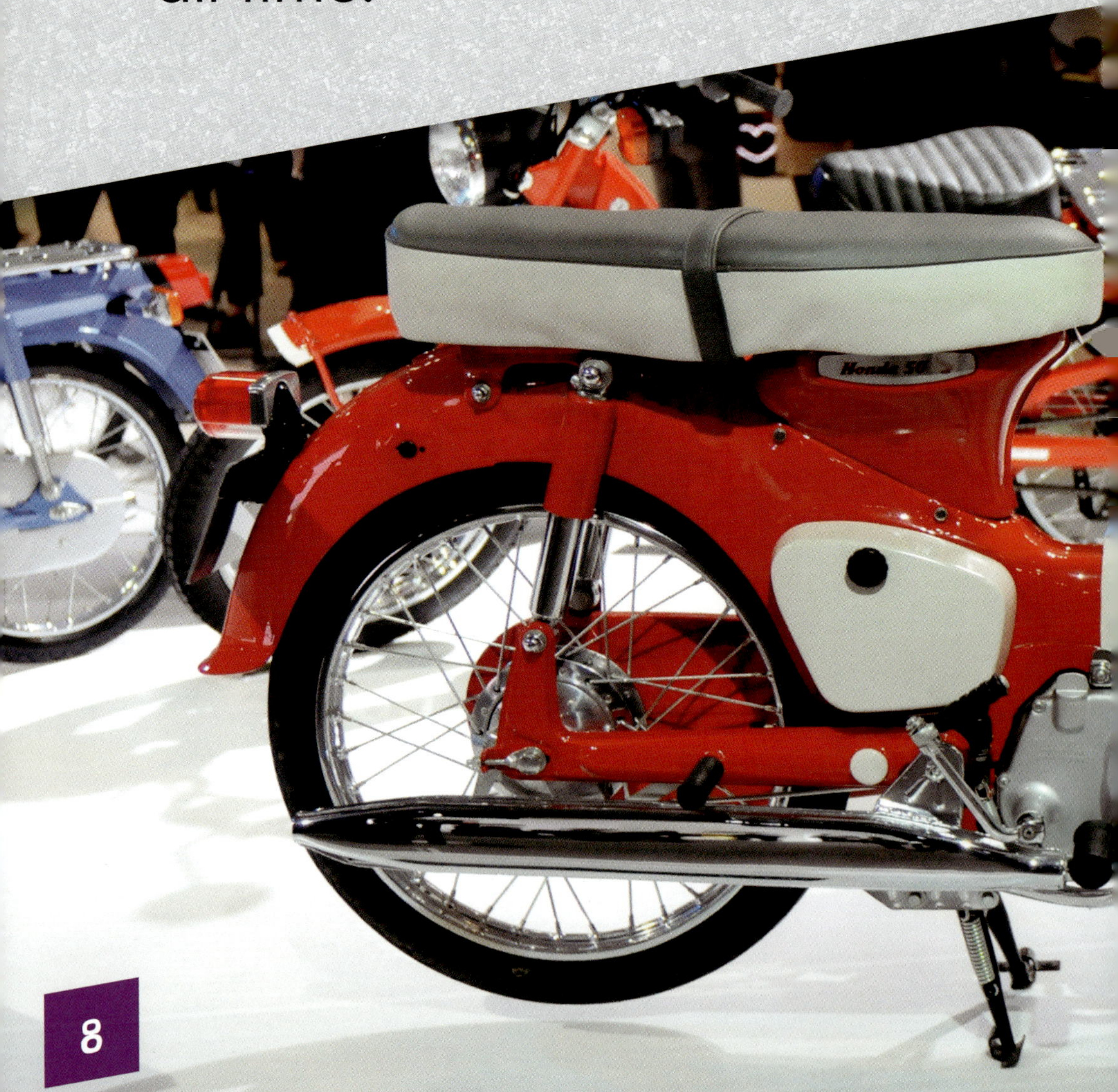

HONDA

The CBR1100XX Super Blackbird came out in 1996. It was the world's fastest motorcycle at the time.

The first Gold Wing was made it 1975. It is a popular **touring** motorcycle.

HONDA

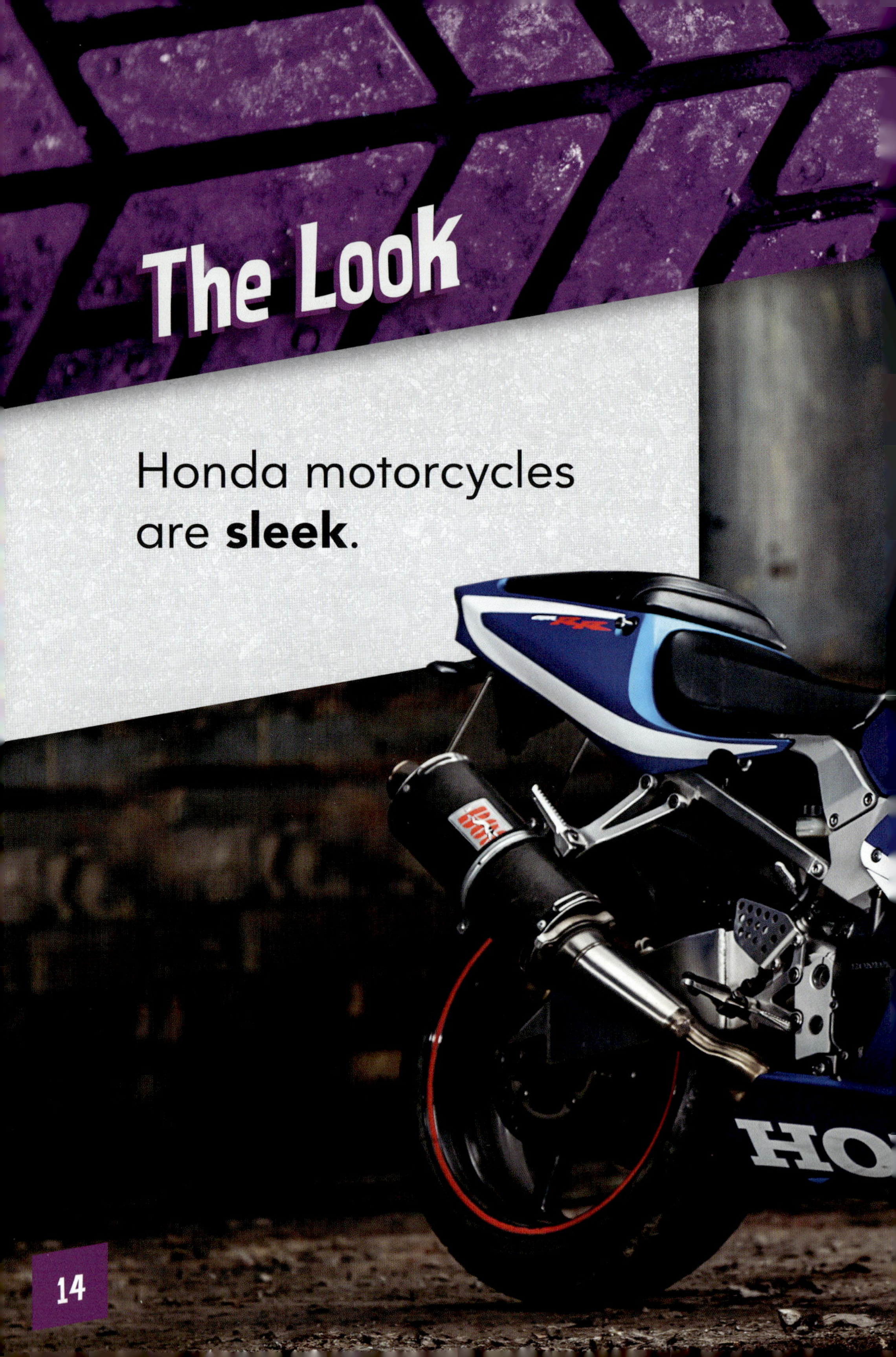

The Look

Honda motorcycles are **sleek**.

HONDA
FireBlade
NDA

Honda introduced a **4-stroke** engine in 1951. It was quiet, smooth, and **dependable**.

HONDA
CBR

Some Hondas are made for trail riding. The CRF450X has been called an "off-road warrior."

REPSOL
LOTUS
SHOEI
GIVES YOU WINGS
LOTUS
GAS
93
REPSOL
HONDA
REPSOL
HONDA

Honda is big in racing. **Grand Prix** motorcycle champ Marc Márquez has taken first place many times on his Honda RC213V.

More Facts

- Honda makes more motorcycles than any other company.

- Over 100 million Super Cubs have been made.

- Honda holds many motorcycle racing records.

Glossary

dependable – able to be counted on.

four-stroke – an engine in which the piston completes four separate strokes while turning the crankshaft.

Grand Prix – a major race held each year that takes place on a long, difficult course.

sleek – trim and graceful lines.

touring – a motorcycle designed to keep a rider comfortable for longer rides.

Index

Online Resources

To learn more about Honda, please visit **abdobooklinks.com**. These links are routinely monitored and updated to provide the most current information available.